Sound the Shofar!

A Story for ROSH HASHANAH and YOM KIPPUR

written by Leslie Kimmelman

pictures by John Himmelman

HarperCollins*Publishers*

Special thanks to Cantor Julie Yugend-Green
and Karen Beitel

Library of Congress Cataloging-in-Publication Data
Kimmelman, Leslie.
   Sound the shofar! : a story for Rosh Hashanah and Yom Kippur / by
Leslie Kimmelman ; illustrated by John Himmelman.
      p.   cm.
   Summary: Uncle Jake gets to blow the shofar twice within ten days, as the
family celebrates first Rosh Hashanah and then Yom Kippur.
   ISBN 0-06-027501-4.
   [1. Shofar–Fiction.   2. Rosh ha-Shanah–Fiction.   3. Yom Kippur–Fiction.
4. Fasts and feasts–Judaism–Fiction.   5. Jews–United States–Fiction.
6. Uncles–Fiction.]   I. Himmelman, John, ill.   II. Title.
PZ7.K56493So   1998   96-45027
[E]–dc21   CIP
                                                  AC

7 8 9 10
❖

To Alex and Emily—
may all your years be good and sweet
—L.K.

For Temple Beth Shalom
—J.H.

My uncle Jake blows the shofar every day.
He is practicing to play at synagogue for
the coming holidays, the Days of Awe.

The Days of Awe begin with Rosh Hashanah,
the Jewish New Year.
My relatives all come to visit
and share our delicious dinner.

My mother lights the holiday candles.

My father blesses the wine.

Everyone takes a piece of challah.

My grampa dips his piece in honey.

"Shanah Tovah," he says. "May it

be a good and sweet year."

My cousins dip apple slices in honey.

The cats lick honey drops from the floor.

The sweet new year is beginning already!

After dinner, and during

the next two days, we go to synagogue.

The rabbi leads us in prayer,

and the cantor leads us in song.

Finally, it's the moment

I've been waiting for.

Uncle Jake goes

to the front of the room.

He picks up the shofar

and blows it over and over.

Listen, everyone!

The New Year is beginning!

But Uncle Jake can't rest yet.

Yom Kippur comes ten days
after Rosh Hashanah, and he will
blow the shofar again.

On Yom Kippur, grown-ups don't eat at all,
and we kids eat only a little.
But the cats eat the same as always.

We go to synagogue in the morning.

My aunts bring cans of tuna fish.

We are collecting food for families

who don't have enough to eat.

The synagogue is crowded all day.

We spend the day praying and thinking.

We think about the year that's ending

and the one that's just beginning.

We remember all the things
we wish we hadn't done.
I remember pulling my cat's tail.

My brother remembers
squeezing the whole tube
of toothpaste into the bathroom sink.

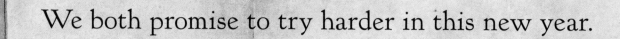
We both promise to try harder in this new year.

At last, the holiday is almost over.

Uncle Jake picks up the shofar again.

He blows the horn, loud and sweet.

The Days of Awe have come to an end.

Shanah Tovah!

THE DAYS OF AWE

Every year, early in the fall, Jewish people all around the world celebrate ten special days called the Days of Awe, or the High Holy Days. The Days of Awe begin with Rosh Hashanah, the Jewish New Year, and end with Yom Kippur, the Day of Atonement. They are quiet days, for thinking about the past year and praying for help to do better. They are good days for saying "I'm sorry" for all the mistakes that were made.

On Rosh Hashanah, a special meal is prepared. Sweet foods such as honey, raisins, carrots, and apples are eaten in the hope that the new year will be filled with sweetness. At synagogue, the *shofar*, or ram's horn, is sounded over and over, calling everyone to attention–just as Jews blew the shofar thousands of years ago to call their people together.

On Yom Kippur, more people go to synagogue than at any other time of the year. The very first sound that is heard on the eve of the holiday is the voice of the cantor, singing a very old, very beautiful prayer called the *Kol Nidre*. All through Yom Kippur, Jews pray for forgiveness, from each other and from God. They promise to find ways to become better people. Most Jews over the age of thirteen don't eat or drink during Yom Kippur. That keeps their minds and bodies free to pray to God. And being hungry is a reminder to help others who are often hungry and cold. Many synagogues collect food or clothing to give away to those in need.

At the end of the day, the shofar is sounded one last time. The Days of Awe are over. A new year–maybe the best ever!–is beginning.